THIS IS WHY WE MET

A POEM COLLECTION ON DATING, FRIENDS WITH BENEFITS & SEX WORKERS

By Chris Statham

Also By

THE UGLY GLORY SERIES

THE MAN IN THE MIRROR - A collection on male mental health
FRIDAY NIGHT FEVER – A collection on booze, nightlife & the battle with sobriety
JELLIED EELS & MULTI-CULTURALISM – A collection on modern life in the UK
THIS IS WHY WE MET - A collection on dating, friends with benefits & sex workers
MY NORTH STAR - A collection on love, divorce & finding a way forward
JUST ANOTHER MARTIAN CAT LIVING IN BASILDON - A collection on exploring creativity & the world
LIFE PIRATE – A collection on life, death & all that jazz

AFRONIA SERIES

Crying for Afronia (Volume 1)
Escape from Afronia (Volume 2)
Dying for Afronia (Volume 3)
Afronia Rising (Volume 4)
Developing Afronia (Volume 5)

PROSE, POEM AND PICTURES SERIES

7 Days in 1 Week (Volume 1)
12 Months in a Year (Volume 2)
10 Years in a Decade (Volume 3)

OTHER FICTION NOVELS

18 Reflections and 3 Statements of Relief
Paperback Writer

DEDICATION

To lovers past, present and future

Copyright and Disclaimer

Author – Chris Statham
Sketches by Hezdean Chinthengah
Published by **www.creativityxroads.com**
THIS IS WHY WE MET, 978-1-7385368-0-1

CONTENTS

Contents

FORWARD

Question: what makes us human? Answer: sex... and a few other things. I was reading the other day, in 10,000 years' time, give or take, the human species may split in two sub-species. The underclass "runt goblins" will be bred out, whereas "superhumans" would be: seven-footers, athletic like Michael Johnson, more intelligent than Stephen Hawking, creative geniuses like Michelangelo, have a chin Dan Dare would be proud of and, be as long dicked as a porn star. As for the super ladies, they will be hairless Amazonians boasting breasts like the ripest of mangoes and an ass capable of cracking walnuts. However, the fly in the ointment to this prediction... robots will observe us as antiquated playthings.

Back to sex, one of the most fundamental aspects of our humanity. Regardless of colour, creed, religion or sexual preference, men and women shag. It's not only a pleasurable experience but also healthy. It reduces stress and you get a high from the release of the hormone oxytocin, the so-called "love drug". For the ladies- a good rogering can make an early menopause less likely. In summary, more sex = less sickness due to higher levels of the antibody immunoglobulin. And, apparently, it makes your cleverer, this according to research into oldies. As such, I suggest openly sharing past sex lives with new partners. There should be no shame. It can be liberating, arousing for some, to hear about another's past erotic encounters.

On a similar topic, porn; it's messing with the melons of many, especially men. Everyone has fantasies and porn is a visualised outlet for what will never happen. In a society heavily influenced by image-based social media, it's not surprising many grapple with physical insecurities. Increasing numbers feel inadequate in comparison with porno actors and suffer from performance anxiety, viewers not able to match the Ken and Barbie fantasy bodies and athleticism of pixelated gymnastic porn stars.

Sex, an integral aspect of our humanity, encompasses a broad spectrum of experiences and which are explored through this collection of poems. No topic is considered taboo with an understanding that sex maybe lead to positive or negative experiences, though should always be consensual. These poems delve into diverse avenues through which sex may manifest, whether initiated or enabled by a hook-up app, be borne out of friends with benefits or, chance encounters and old-fashioned serendipity. It acknowledges the significant difference between cheating, dating and the many grey areas in-between. Why some men and women drop their trousers at the first opportunity and eagerly shed their inhibitions, whereas others remain stubbornly belt-buckled and retain a steadfast restraint. It explores the diverse flavours of sexual experiences from the so-called "vanilla" to the kinky and which is ultimately only constrained to a person's imagination and a willingness to push their and their partner's boundaries. Additionally, these poems candidly address the multifaceted reasons underlying prostitution, examining the perspectives of both buyers and providers, irrespective of gender.

DATING & THE APP HOOK UP

I suppose when there's so much sex-on-tap with the avalanche of hook-up apps, maybe it's not surprising singletons and those partnered-up contemplate their options. The prevalence of romance algorithms is now deciding our sex lives. This is utterly depressing on almost every level and just one more aspect of technology governing our daily existence. It begs the question, what's happened to happenstance, aligning of the stars, chance and living to the sound of randomness and chaos? Now we're all cogs in a well-oiled machine, our relationships commoditized and governed by lines of code. Are we already living in the Matrix? On the other hand...

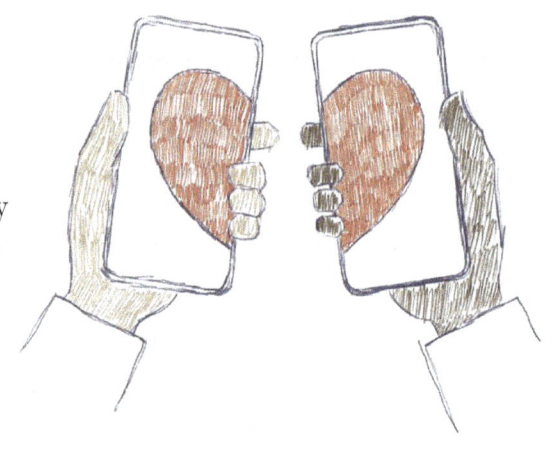

The Whim of Quim

Big girls,
small girls,
I'm calling all girls;
sex and life,
a fucking mystery.

What is it that makes men go crazy,
doolally,
become pussy whipped?

A physical attraction,
interaction,
emotional contraction,
our monkey brains programmed to need female
curves.

Boobs we suckled on,
vagina we came from,
men,
destined to search for where we arrived,
but not the 1 in 10...
the squeezing ass percentile,
men's not women's

Big girls,
small girls,

I'm calling all girls;
sex and life,
a fucking mystery.

She's small,
cute,
not an inch to pinch,
a petite with flat chest,
tight pussy;
a girl you can pick up and fuck standing,
porno staring.

The big girl with a big ass,
big belly,
big tits who fucks all night,
a real goer,

willing and wanting to do anything,
happy for the dick love.

The tall one,
striking and she knows it,
out of your league apart from the one night,
you on fire,
can sell snow to an eskimo,
hit the jackpot you think,
but she is no gas,
laugh,
a fantastic fuck in your minds-eye,
one to remember…
but boring,
only one fuck,
can't get hard for a second,
not like four times with fatty,
five with the little'un.

The average,
like you.
Not full of herself but good fun,
a good shag and happy days,
potential soulmate.

The quiet-
this a short stanza,
don't know this girl,
not been with one,
not my type of woman.

The dirty-
she knows it,
you want it,
hugely excited by it,
living your fantasies,
perversions,

desires and craziness,
the one who never says, no.

Girls,
all shapes and sizes,
minds and means,
each living their reality as I'm living mine.

Big girls,
small girls,
I'm calling all girls;
sex and life,
a fucking mystery.

Tall or short,
fat or thin,
everyone a win.

Checkout boobs and ass,
a handful to clasp,
but pussy
punani…
whether gerbil's ass or wizard sleeve,
a single finger or whole fist,
hidden behind skirt or shorts,
g-string or granny pants,
a woman's secret is a man's desire,
a coming together of freedom,
acceptance,
a meeting of minds.

Big girls,
small girls,
I'm calling all girls;
sex and life,
a fucking mystery.

25-Year Old Virgin

I'm 25 and not fucked,
not even a dick suck or clit lick.

I get turned on,
am a pussy tease,
let him rub between my legs,
dry hump me,
finger my ass…
but I'm not giving up my fanny tonight.

This is my choice,
my body,
my decision when to pop my cherry,
with who,
how,
where and when I want;
respect that,
bitch!

I go on a first date,
we smile and chat,
drink,
but not too much,
work tomorrow.

I'm a sensible girl,
don't get drunk,
high or fuck around.

I live with my parents,
obey rules,
back home before late…
not being a free woman doing what I want.

Culture dictates my life,
my body staying virgin.
I'm not waiting for marriage but can't find the
right man,
they all boys,
no one makes me rebel,
can get me to say-
fuck you life and rules,
fuck you mum, dad and religion,

I'm a grown ass woman,
working,
flirting when I want,
fucking if I desire.

Allow me to live,
to love,
to suck and fuck if I want,
when, where and with who.

None of you are my god but a chain round my
wrists and ankles,
and not the good type,
I, wanting to be tied up.

You think I'm your pension,
that I should look after you rather than live.
You are hypocrites,
me,
your first born conceived out of wedlock…
when drunk…
and high….
and no condom….
get over yourself!

I'm not angry,
I just want respect,
to live my life as a free woman.

Tinder Fate

I was meant to be with my ex,
my sister from another mister,
a soul who we connected,
laughter and fun times,
fate getting in the way.

I was meant to be with my friend with benefits,
we met,
had a laugh,
she overstepped boundaries,
things got messed up,
fate got in the way.

That's life,
I swipe to the right,
to the left,
a star for a hot girl,
cross for not.

I get the same treatment…
a half-second decision,
nothing about me,
who I am,
where I've been or what I'm about.

A picture to decide,
to conclude,
to come to a swipe decision,
a thoughtlessness,
a sliding-doors moment
to decide if we will meet,
talk,
fuck.

If denied,
neither of us will experience the vibe of experimentation,
uncertainty and what ifs.
Living the known,
the safe
preferring this to the unknown,
than unexpected.

But tonight I'm feeling good,
fly,
ready for now,
for a night of dating as I go to meet my Tinder.

I'm set up,
no longer hung up,
hopefully to get tied up;
is my life about to get fucked up?

I see her,
our eyes lock –
wariness,
flirtatiousness,
excitement all in one;
I'm ready for love,
a lust journey.

We approach,
touch hands,
electricity goes through my mind.

We sit down,
order drinks,
chat,
smile and tell truths;
the night just starting.

Things don't work out
fate that brought us together
now dividing'
So,
back out there on the dating trail,
a Tinder finder,
not sure what life will bring,
sorrow more than joy in my heart;
will fate get in the way or open a new door?

I swipe to the right,
to the left,
a star for a hot girl,
cross for not.

I know I get the same treatment...
a half second of decision,
probably derision,
nothing about me,
who I am,
where I've been,
what I'm about.

A picture to decide,
to conclude,
come to a swipe decision,

a thoughtless moment in time deciding if we
meet,
talk,
fuck or cry,
a sliding-doors moment.

A new meet,
date.
I hear about her boyfriend,
she my drama,
we friends,
not sexual,
not now.

But there's a vibe of experimentation,
uncertainty,
hopes,
what ifs but not now,
both preferring the known to the unknown,
the safe to the unexpected,
potential friendship,
who knows if more,
if stars will be reached or spaceships crashed.

Fate will decide what comes next.
I'm not chasing,
remembering-
I'm a life pirate,
fate steering,
I'm the captain of the ship.

Tinder Date

I'm nor the richest man,
and… belly protruding,
grey hairs sprouting,
but I'm also a stallion galloping,
never breaking,
hopefully always interesting.

Log on to Tinder,
looking for fun and friends,
nothing serious;
bonus frolics maybe.

A Tinder date,
tried a few before
never got anywhere,
always a waste of time and energy.

Not quite true…
one time,
thought meeting a girl for date,
ended up massage parlour,
the most sensual ever,
extras worth paying for.

But tonight,
hoping,
expecting flirting and fucking,
drinking and partying,
making a new friend,
with benefits or not,
this, the joy of dating.

Meet Sara at the agreed place and time;
what a beauty.

Not a young girl,
immature,
money-grabbing,
but a proper woman,
grown,
knows herself and understands me.

I tell of my crazy,
egg-shotting self,
the being myself,
me,
no pretence,
no intense,
just the beer drinking,
hard working travelling me.

I'm being honest,
nothing to lose,
friend or fuck,
boredom or laughter,
it's all good,
she an actor in my life story.

This is Tinder land,
each night a new experience,
reality,
possible futility,
probable finality,
if good,
hopefully repeatability.

Tinder Toilet

Sad and lonely,
feeling horny,
needing friendship more than fuck buddy,
but extras…
would be extra pleasing.

Fire up the smartphone,
crack open the dating app,
no messages.
Swipe right,
right,
right and right again.

Five minutes and thirty minutes more,
a message,
hope.

We chat,
text flirt,
agree to meet up.

Drinks are drunk,
stories told,
she thinks I'm too bold.

Laughter had
kisses laid,
can't wait
connection made and toilet visited,
bodies ignite.

Go to bed,
reunite,
new friend found,
both living our experience.

Tinder Fail

We said 7:30,
it's now past 8.
Come on, man,
be reasonable,
honest,
give me a reason,
an excuse…
a new estimated time on arrival.

Life happens,
things get delayed,
we all know that but be human,
show respect,
make apologies when late,
this common courtesy,
a reasonable mind,
being a reasonable person.

It's the arrogance,
the not caring,
the narcissism,

I'm near fuming,
she finally coming,
giving no excusing.

She pretty,
a little ity bitty,
but mind shitty,
boring,
make me snoring,
want to go exploring,
find exciting,
not more time-wasting,
pointless tasting,
she sugar no spice,
this not nice,
bland,
predictable and wasting my time.

Stood Up

A chance meeting,
a brief encounter,
I thought we clicked,
mutual attraction,
fascination.

Phones numbers swapped,
messages exchanged,
meet up planned,
a night to know each other,
adventures to be explored,
fun times had.

Arrive at the agreed location,
at the agreed time,
anticipation and hope running through veins.

I wait,
my arms getting chilly,
the beer bottle emptying,
the evening not getting started,
the date not lighted;
have you stood me up?

Thirty minutes,
one hour,
three poems,
four beers and you're still not here.

No good excuse,
no logical explanation,
no courtesy,
nothing but lies,
nonsensical reasons for your lateness,
devilish variants to the expected reality;
why?

Don't fuck me around.
I'm not playing games,
I have enough shit to deal with,
don't need another dump plopping onto my
plate.

What sort of person thinks this way?
your word is your bond,
pension and personality!
Who the fuck do you think you are?
Do you think I'm a fool,
have no worth or self-control?

This is rudeness,
utmost crudeness,
inconsideration.

I don't want to be your friend,
I don't live a life of desperation.

I don't need you in my life;
good luck,
goodbye and fuck off!

I leave more annoyed than destroyed,
pissed-off,
possibilities not given a chance;
This is life,
being stood up one more life experience to my
collection.

Second Chances

We met once
twice;
will there be a thrice?

The first time,
chance encounter,
energy and enthusiasm,
chemistry,
enjoy the serendipity,
randomness,
swap numbers and keep contact.

The second time,
you arrive late,
very,
the opposite of courtesy,
I'm pissed off,
night ok but not rocking,
no interest rolling,
going with the flow,
too much annoyance,
drunkenness.

Despite it all we stay in contact.
For me,
I love your energy,
rawness,
can't give a fuckness.

You have demons as I have mine,
whatever might be between us,
whether something or nothing,
it will not be boring.

We will go down in flames or reach highs of
passion,
our relationship will not be whimpering,
pussy footing,
hopefully pussy licking,
dick sucking,
ass slapping,
spitting and biting,
hard banging,
penetrating,
good fucking,
explosive riding,
penetrating,
lost in the momenting...
but more likely nothing.

I have to decide...
will we meet a third time?

The Health Clinic?

What did I do?
Who did I do?
Why did I do it?

Pain shooting through my magic stick,
a cloudy, sticky ooze on the tip,
this the after party come down.

Bite the bullet,
see the doc.
cross my fingers,
pray to Jesus,
Mohammed,
Buddha and Lord Krishna,

The nurse calls me from the waiting-room,
a look of bored resignation on her face.
She has seen 1,000 worried men like me before,
all scared of our stupidity,
impulsivity,
drunken revelry.

"Come back tomorrow,"
I'm told;
what does this mean?

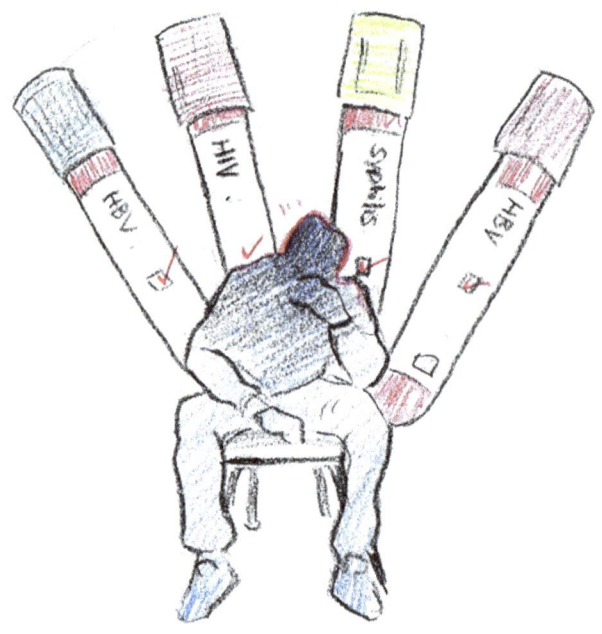

"Nothing to worry about,"
I'm advised.
"Take these tablets,"
I'm handed as I leave,
my mind pondering the current reality,
hoping no lasting effects of crazy carnality.

KINKY SEX

Sexual exploration and experimentation are deeply personal experiences. Have you ever had kinky sex, experimented and done every perverted thing you ever fantasised with your partner, spouse, friend or sex-worker? Are you too afraid to ask? Have you been going at it hammer and tongs, when someone revealed their sexual peccadillos? It could be spanking, submission, anal, tied up, dominance, pegging… if you can think of it there will be a name! Besides, what is normal sex? Who says there should be rules and regulations as to what's permissible or acceptable so long as there's consent? Sexual preferences and practices are highly subjective and quite

rightly there is no list of do's and don'ts. What might seem odd, kinky or guilt-inducing to you might be fundamental carnal pleasure to someone else! As long as it's consensual, I say, anything goes that gets both to orgasm. While it is essential to establish boundaries, by having honest conversations about desires, fantasies, and potential kinks or fetishes with your partner(s), then mutual pleasure and satisfaction can be achieved for all parties!

Sometimes Tender Sometimes Rough

My girl,
my love,
my princess,
my everything.

My treat tenderly,
kiss all over,
massage with feeling,
lick where she likes,
do what she wants-
I'm her slave.

My bitch,
my whore,
my cock slut,
my treat you how I want.

I'll spit on you,
massage you with dick in your ass,
slap you when I desire,
bite where it hurts,
you'll do what I want,
you are my slave.

Sex is all about passion and feeling,
and anger,
and desire,
and hate,
and insecurity,
and neediness,
and happiness,
and depression,
and laughter,
and self-loathing,
and expectation,

and condoms,
and periods,
and excitement,
and excrement,
and restrained,
and blindfolds,
and no rules,
and the unknown,
and too well known,
and exchange of fluids,
and money,
and resolved,
and retribution,
and fantasy,
and clothes removed,
and leather,
and nakedness,
and revealing your soul,
and fetish,
and no rules,
and blow jobs,
and fucking,
and giving,
and taking,
and panting,
and lost in the moment,
and cunnilingus,
and sex toys,
and longing,
and, and, and…

We are human heads with hearts of animals who
need love,
sometimes tender sometimes rough,
always together, never enough.

Threesome

A cum stain from porn overload,
a fantasy only found in wet dreams,
a reality not often,
but life-affirming when it happens.

Whether with friends or lovers,
those you pay,
sharing a bed with two others,
magical.

You are a king for an hour,
a night.
There is no other feeling like fucking one girl
while kissing,
licking,
fingering another.

Threesomes,
a moment,
an experience that everyone should have at least
once.
It's all physical,
mental,
emotional feelings switched to full.

And I expect the same for girls,
two dicks better than one,
being treated as a goddess or whore,

LGBTQ+ friends,
everyone deserves to live temet nosce,
to the fullest,
to experience sexual magic and have a threesome.

Unrestrained

Mouth smiling,
boobs popping,
legs spreading,
you are my bitch.

Cock erecting,
lips licking,
trousers dropping,
you are my bitch.

Clothes disrobing,
skin shinning,
nipples standing,
you are my bitch.

Teeth biting,
hands gliding,
pussy wetting,
you are my bitch.

Back laying,
face slapping,
mouth spitting,
you are my bitch.

Ass spreading,
dick pissing,
my pretty drinking,
you are my bitch.

Eyes blindfolding,
body whipping,
candle dripping,
you are my bitch.

Hands restraining,
spread-eagling,
throat choking,
you are my bitch.

I'm entering,
cunt squirting,
I'm cumming,
you are my bitch.

Kinky Sex

I close my eyes,
porn reality…

My girl,
my bitch,
my friend the freak handcuffed,
spread-eagled,
giving herself to my desires,
defenceless.

Drip a candle,
rub with an ice cube,
insert something other than my dick into pussy,
ass;
she can't resist,
complain,
cry out…
due to the ball-gag in her mouth.

When eyes lock,
I see excitement of the unknown,
fear of the unknown,
all that she's been told is wrong…
is what she craves.

When she shakes her head,
moans in pain,
tries to say, no,
she means, yes.

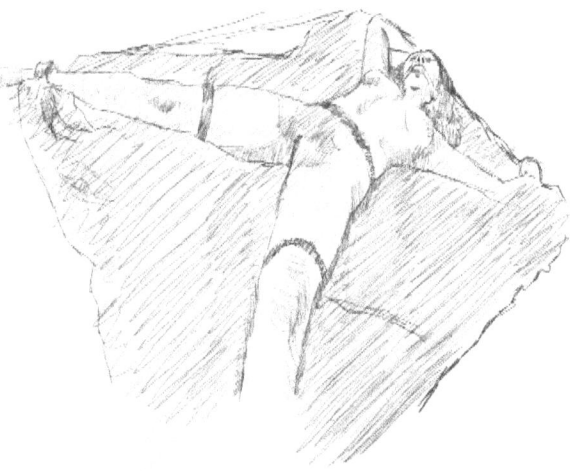

She's a rebel to the ordinary,
a woman free with her sexuality
who lives for the now,
to get lost in the moment,
to obey her master,
to be a sexualised puppet,
a deviant to my whim.

Anal

Part 1

He's cute,
he's cool;
fancy him,
digging on all that.

Got me laughing,
panty wetting,
soon shagging,

pussy destroying,
I'm hoping!

He fuck good,
dick probing,
clit licking,
I'm cumming,
he want my ass spreading,
I'm not giving.

What's that with guys?
Why do they want anal,
my vag not tight enough?

My ass is mine,
not given before and you're not fucking it tonight.

I don't know why....
culture or couture,
nature or nurture;
I'm not into anal torture.

Leave my ass alone!
It's dirty,
aren't I crazy enough for you?

Have my mouth and puss,
anytime,
all the time,
but you're not getting my ass,
I, no three-hole girl.

Part 2

I'm an ass man,
love that squeeze,
pulling apart and tonguing that tight little hole.

I'll fuck a pussy or mouth,
but anal,
that holds a special place in my heart.

Why?

Is it...
once past first base pussy is guaranteed,
the question,
will the woman give her ass?

Has she given it before,
this a sign of mental freedom,
a stronger connection,
or she a brown starfish virgin,
I,
the first to enter an exclusive club!

Perhaps,
if she takes it in the ass,
up the Gary Glitter,
shitter,
what other dirty,
sex crazy,
mad frenzy,
kinky fucking will we do?

Is it psychological?
I've an ass and could get if fucked,
man-on-man or dominatrix pegging;
I need to know,
want to feel what it's like.

All I know,
I love a lass with a good ass,
and ass is something that I like,
love.

STREET HOOKERS & MASSAGE PARLOURS

The topic of paying for sex is complex and multifaceted. Do you have moral outrage at those who pay for sex? Do you think paying for sex is unhealthy and exploitative, that transactions objectify and dehumanize individuals or, that some (mainly men) just want the company?

Different perspectives exist regarding its moral implications, views varying widely. One friend told me, he looked after his invalid mum and so didn't have much time or opportunity to socialise. He therefore decided to pay a woman to come around and have dinner with him. They would laugh and argue like old friends and sometimes have sex; it was a relationship that suited them both. A second scenario, some women don't like sex that much. The man has no intention of starting an affair but goes with prostitutes to satisfy his needs. What about if the person isn't getting their kinks at home?

Whether golden showers, anal, pegging, bondage etc. some will pay rather than live in forever frustration, Lastly, don't kid yourself, women also pay for sex. Maybe not as many as men, but some quite rightly have no qualms about i t; gigolos are more efficient than cruising bars looking for men to shag. I say, as long as all parties involved are consenting adults and the transaction is conducted safely, paying for / being paid for sex is a legitimate personal choice. There shouldn't be outrage and generalizations but rather an understanding of the nuances.

Buy Me

A loaf of bread or jam doughnut,
buy me also.
Condoms in a pharmacy,
beer in every store,
why not buy me?

Buy a tram ticket,
five fruit and two veg,
pet food…
buy me also.

Pencils sharpened and exercise books,
wherever you go,
whichever shop you might enter,
everything is for sale…
and so am I.

I am on the street,
this my home,
darkness my natural habitat.

Alcohol and sex,
so present in my past,
this my now,
I expect my future also,
everything,
me,
a commodity that has its price.

To some,
whether John or hooker.
I live the unthinkable
others, the ordinary;
I say,
I'm living honesty in its most pure form.

In this world of lies,
deceit,
Facebook pretending,
Instagram famous,
being not who you are,
be your true self,
don't be shy of paying for sex and buying me
Consider work...
yours or mine,

people you share a building,
sit with for 8,10 or more hours,
but what do you know of your colleagues or they
you?
Most hide the truth of messy lives.

Family?
Christmas dinners and false bonhomie,
fake smiles for a few hours;
please,
pull the other cracker!

Religion,
praying to a god in the hope of eternal salvation,
few willing to make the sacrifices demanded to
live by the Word,
kidding themselves there's something more,
a hereafter.

The world full of untruths.
Many say,
you're not a man if you have to pay for sex,
but they prefer porn,
live in denial of their true sexual selves.

Us women or gigolos,
this is a life of choice,
making a living,
doing what we can in a world of supply and
demand.

Prostitution,
an honest exchange of money for sex.
This is my truth,
simplicity,
directness in a world of smoke and mirrors;
BUY ME!

Street Girl

Not been a classic night,
not even that good,
shit to be honest.

Date cancelled,
friends didn't turn up,
no one to talk to,
and booze.
my normally ever faithful companion,
not getting me drunk,
giving me peace.

Time to rest…
but I'm not sleepy.
I've seen glorious smiles,
boob busting tops,
tight asses,
but none of them mine,
not even a touch.

No flirt,
just lonely,
loneliness,
lonesome,
needing to feel fulsome,
if not wholesome.

I start home dispirited,
disappointed,
disinclined to a sunny disposition,
as I want to grab waists,
to be in control,
to feel wanted.

Fuck that,
this is me,
I make rules….
and break them.
If I want a street hooker,
a ten quid fuck,
no one can stop me…
but me.

I will do what I
want,
when I want,
with who I want:
no one tells me,
no.

Screw your
moralising!
Fuck your ethics!
The girl gets paid,
I get brief joy,
sexual satisfaction.

I know it can be
defeating,
all the repeating,
self-hating,
girl paying
sometimes I feel like regurgitating,
but in this moment,
this time,
this very second,
I couldn't care less where she will lead me,
whether guide me to a backstreet room or
quiet corner to fuck.

I will unload my insecurities and anguish,
my mental fragility,
anything to briefly feel better;
I have no care for her thoughts,
her choices leading to street work.

Roxanne

You're not Roxanne.
You're not in the warmth of your bedroom.
There is no red light on your windowsill;
you're a street hooker.

You know each man has demands,
their fetish:
toes, pussy, ass, tits, mouth.
You give it all up for my pleasure,
you'll give anything up for cash,
money that can buy your next fix.

You show legs from under short skirts.
You flash knickers and breasts.
You walk towards me,
hips swaying,
eyes penetrating,
implanting lust in my mind.
Take me,
want me,
fulfil me,
your body tells my brain.

Mister, you say.
Like what you see?
Fancy a good time?
your sales pitch.

I nod mesmerized in hunger,
my mouth unable to form words;
lost in the moment.

I know your life is one of uncertainty,
danger and excitement.
You have sex in a car,
a dark corner,
behind a bush;
in an abandoned warehouse on a flea infested
mattress.

You will sell your body to me,
but not your soul.
I can handcuff and spread-eagle you.
You are my bitch,
my whore,
defenceless;
when you say, no,
I know you mean, yes.

I drip wax onto your naked body.
I insert objects and myself into you.
You don't say anything…
due to the gag in your mouth.
I look into your eyes
and see excitement and worry–
what will I demand next?

There is no romance,
no love,
no feeling
other than a crisp £20 note in your purse.

This is your everyday.
Standing on a corner,
swaying through a nightclub,
a needle in your vein.
You are a hooker,
a street prostitute and will be what I want you to
be,
do what I command.

Little Lady

Little lady,
just 12 years of age but more experienced
than a granny going to the grave in the ways of
men.

Little lady,
left home for a better tomorrow,
across hills and seas you persevered,
men preying on your weakness,
snatching innocence from your body.

Little lady,
sold to the highest bidder,
trafficked..
now legs in the air,
no longer walking to a hopeful future.

Little lady,
you entice lust,
dirty old pervs taking from you,
excited by your innocence,
your unblemished skin,
your freshness.

Little lady,
body aching,
lip split by a John when you refuse to open your
thighs,
raped when you say, no,
beaten by your pimp when you can't face the day
ahead.

Little lady,
you cry…
when you look in the mirror,
when you are forced to get high,
when you drink to forget the pain.

Little lady,
remember your strength,
that you are an angel,

a princess,
that there are good people in this world.

Little lady,
I know you don't want to go out tonight.
it's cold,
wet,
the weather as miserable as your life.

Little lady,
dress well,
your make-up doesn't hide the bruises;
you're fearful but try to show courage.

Little lady,
you are my heroine,
my desire who I will never let go.

Little lady,
you will do what I say or I'll kill you.

Gloryhole

Sex starved,
porn addicted for longer than I care to remember,
care to admit.

Why do I only meet frigid bitches not lose sluts?
Why can't woman accept a pussy is like a dick,
there for pleasure,
not a diamond that needs to be worshipped,
earned?

Why are most women so up themselves?
Why can't they bend over or get on their knees so
I can dump my cum in the whore?

I rather a silly but fun bitch than a girl,
woman,
wife,
witch,
who acts high and mighty,
flighty.

Don't get me wrong-
I love women!
I respect and worship them.
They have a hold over men,
over me;
that's why I fuck prostitutes,
whores, sluts.
With them it's simple,
transactional not emotional;
I get my jollies,
they get paid,
what's the big deal?

There is no commotion,
the only regret,
my self-pity for debasing myself,
feeling lonely,
knowing what we did was fake,
not genuine.

When she turned around while I fucked her from
behind,

thumb in her ass,
her face was plain,
bored.

There was no smile,
vacant eyes telling me of her life,
not what might be.
How, maybe under different circumstances
I could be with a woman who loved me,
ours a passion to rival Romeo and Juliet,
Anthony and Cleopatra.

That is a love that I knew,
that has left my life,
that I don't think I will ever know again from my
ex-wife,
this killing me twice to the bone.

And so I go to a gloryhole,
get a fuck or suck,
no eyes or smiles,
no soothing voice or body to caress,
just a pump, pump, pump explode,
pay,
leave,
relief for fleeting seconds,
in control for mere minutes,

This now my normal as hours,
weeks and months pass until I next go to the
gloryhole,
my mind doing cartwheels thinking of the love I lost.

Extras

I'm married
I'm drunk
I'm pissed off with all the moaning,
whinging,
nit picking,
pocket emptying,
all round bitching,
not appreciating,
feel like regurgitating.

I have it good:
nice job,
kids,
no debt burden,
but I'm dying inside;
I have no one ride or die,
share a life with.

Need someone on my wave length,
not just a marriage certificate signalling end of
freedom,
to try and mould me,
make me someone I'm not.

I'm in financial handcuffs,
she with the keys.
Children responsibilities,
I'm all good with that,
happy to do,
have always done what I need to,
but also let me be me....
if you can't,
the nuclear option,
divorce.

I want to find love once more,
friendship,
companionship,
fucking fun.

I need to feel someone's arms around me,
whether a class girl or street whore,

one-night stand or new soulmate,
I won't differentiate,
each person has own merits,
strengths and weaknesses as do I.

I need to feel better about myself,
to be sexually satisfied,
emotionally connected,
feel I'm living with someone who knows me,
understands me,
my wife left that long ago.

Five beers in,
neither drunk nor sober,
I'm contemplating the night ahead,
empty bed,
so weigh up my options,
not sure what I want other than a woman,
to briefly ease my tormented soul.

Can't be arsed with a bar,
a lounge where I'll be hassled by gold diggers...
sweet smiles but fake news,

I don't want sleep,
not by myself,
not tonight.

I need a woman's body,
a cuddle,
a smile,
someone to share a bed whether for minutes or
hours.

A hooker is a possibility,
but I don't want pure transaction,
prefer connection,
temporary or longer,
a massage,
possibly with extras,
get the frustrations of life out,
ejaculate disappointments.

Pocket short,
decisions to be made;
high class not an option-
so down and dirty,
cheap booze,
cheap girls,
cheap frills it is.

Alcohol and sex
two fundamentals to the psyche of men like me,
this my reality,
part of who I am,
my monkey brain looking for acceptance,
chemical reactions,
to find a mate.

Taxi Money

I'm a man and woman are my choice;
any woman can get a man,
but only if we say yes,
we almost always do.

I walk the street,
hookers showing their wares,
$10 for a side-street fuck,
half that for a blowie.

Pass a massage parlour,
beautiful girls able to pleasure,
extras or not.

Enter the nightclub,
fat wallet leads to fat ass in my hands.
Dance and kiss,
push erection into her back,
she shimmering,
panting,
start negotiating,
she wanting paying.

Go to a classy joint,
beauty around,
girls choose you,
make you feel lucky to chat them,
honoured to buy their drinks,
anything they desire;
it's a girl's world,
men, their simple pawns,
always paying.

Jokes shared,
phone number swapped,
we meet at hers;
game on-
an open goal.

Take bottle of wine,
two,
act a gentleman and play it cool,
interested....
but not too much,
not desperate.

Joke,
drink a few,
smoke shisha,
surreptitiously rub boobs-
both know what's about to happen.

I like you,
she says.
I need respect,
understanding;
I work a poorly paid job.

I've heard it all before,
wasn't expecting it tonight.

If you can help me,
support me,
I would be grateful.
My last boyfriend took advantage.
He stayed at my flat,
ate my food,
had my body....
didn't support me...
you understand.

I understand....
wrap it up however you want-
plutonic friendship or transactional,
I'm reactional,

this not what I signed up for,
not who I thought she was,
what I'm looking for.

Finish drink and smoke,
the night past midnight,
I drunk and horny,
limited options so share a bed.

Clothes disrobed,
have some fun but heart not in it,
mind not free-flowing,
even Viagra not working.

The morning comes,
we will not bed again,
another tick on the life journey-
every night like a box of chocolates...
you never know what you'll get.

Disappointed but not defeated,
deflated,
hope still burning eternal,
tonight to the nightclub.

A shorty catches my attention,
quickly to flirtation,
talk and connection made,
hope about to get laid.

I pay drinks and food,
this cheaper,
longer time than a hooker,
less disappointing than last night,
but not satisfying.

It's all a bit weird,
neither good nor bad,
two lost souls trying to get thru life,
looking for brief company;
I'll give her taxi money in the morning.

Pub Hooker

I hope,
I try to be attractive in mind, body and soul,
exciting to the opposite sex.
sometimes it works,
more often not.

I have no idea why one-day green light,
when normally a forest of reds.
Attraction is utterly baffling,
why only sometime reaction?
This leads to mind disturbed,
mentally perturbed.

Fuck it!
I'm fucked up,
hammered,
drunk and can barely stand.

I want a drink,
a chat,
not to be sold something,
somebody;
I'm a grown man and know what I'm doing,
less so after a few scheberts.

I'm susceptible to womanly charms,
easy in hooker bars,
simple,
straight-forward,
women not pretending to be something they're
not.
There's not manipulating,
fake crying,
too much lying,
that's all back at home.

I go to a bar,
ladies of the night plying their trade,
having a drink,
not bothering me while giving the hustle,
waiting for you,
the punter,

John to make the first move,
decide which girl you want,
fat or thin,
tall or short,
attitude or innocent,
tight ass or big boobs;
too much pussy to be disappointed,
it might not be the girl I'm looking for,
but any hole is the goal and I'll pay,
I'm tired of being mentally disjointed.

I look across the room,
a distance not far but chasm between desire and
touch.

The dress extenuates her curves,
fishnet stockings are held on by lace garter.
I'm in horny limbo,
wanting,
but not able to reach.

She walks towards me,
hips swaying,
eyes penetrating,
lust on her mind,
I, soon to be putty in her hands.

Mister,
you like what you see?
she enquires,
flirts,
makes clear her intentions.

I nod mesmerised,
unable to form words,
lost in the moment
at the vision in front that orders:
want me,
take me,
fulfil me...
you will be my plaything.

She sits next to me,
hand moving up my thigh,
I calculating what finance is needed to acquire
her services.

I'm a stranded,
gasping fish at the end of her line,
her whim will decide my immediate future.

It takes three drinks and two negotiations to
agree, but I'm horny and you're beautiful,
maybe not in the light of day,
but now,

tonight,
you Beyoncé and I Timberlake.
I, a handsome witty genius,
you a goddess.

I want my hole,
that my only goal,
to forget the world,
alcohol only partly helping.

I need a woman,
you,
I will get over the ex by getting under you,
You under my brief control,
this what my money gets,
I bending the will of the world,
not being bent.

I saw beds behind the shebeen,
dirty and dank,
sweat stained and cum encrusted,
but for twenty minutes-
more if I can last-
it will be our love palace,
as I romance you,
entrance you,
take you to heaven and back,
the best fuck you've ever had...
and I know you've had. a lot,
probably two already tonight!

Now is time to forget,
relent,
as I leave my worries for the morrow.

Flashing Lights

I know not where I'm going,
I'm in no rush to get there;
I have time,
my destination where fate takes me.

"Hey, mister",
a girl shimmies towards,
giving knowing smile,
points to flashing lights.

Curiosity raised,
I must investigate.

As I get closer I hear music;
no harm going in,
what's the worst that can happen?

Greeted by a hostess,
my mind re-evaluates as I walk downstairs,
my inquisitiveness rising.

I enter a small bar,
a smart place,
good décor,
nice music but few people.

A random Christmas tree-
the source of the flashing lights-
in the corner;
I'm momentarily confused.

Two bar girls,
prostitutes approach.

They're out of luck,
no free drink from me;
I'm in poemathon mode,
this my sixth.

Look around,
see a pole,
a dancing girl moving,

grooving,
riding and smiling,
so enticing,
titillating.

Halfway through my beer –
what'll come first?
The bottom of my bottle,
this poem,
me…
hands now exploring in shorts.

Four more sips,
beer finished,
the girl smiles,
licks her lips,
"Buy me a drink,"
she seductively orders,
a transactional offer.

I'm tempted…
until I remember my missus;
I don't want trouble.

I finish,
pray my daughter will never work a bar,
conclude this poem…

Alfonza

Walking the beach,
sand creeping through toes,
I marvel at the enormity of life,
of the night sky.

I feel at peace,
waiting in anticipation for my next experience,
to feel alive and live my life force.

Neon lights catch my attention –
Club de Fiesta.
I'm reminded of my cold, wet, hometown nightclub,
exotica in a concrete jungle.

My senses are alive as I enter the strip bar,
I've been to many before,
female supply outstripping demand,
where you pay for your pleasure,
desire;
there's no romance,
though debauchery aplenty.

Music is pumping,
lights glowing and girls floating…
but nothing feels exciting,
enticing.

Life is gaudy with no soul.
Electric eyes stare…
but there's no power,
too much fast food,
the girls too easy,
no hunt or chase,
no excitement,
it's boring.

Everything a man can want is on sale,
but there's nothing you can own,
say it's yours,
to love and treasure a good woman,
to admire,
to find a partner in life.

The girls do what they need,
but that's not what I need.
There's no stories or passion,
individualism,
history or discovery here,
just money searching;
any girl available for a price.

Strip bars,
I disgust myself!
Not the objectification of women,
but the lowest denominator of attraction…
paying for a chat.
splurging on human touch;
it's unhealthy interaction.

But…
I like the firecracker with blue dreadlocks.
Alfonza is her name,
boobs bursting outta her bra,
her game.

What goes through that young mind?
Who is she?
Who is he?
Her manager,
pimp…
boyfriend for the evening?

There's no man at this bar who will solve her problems.
There's no dream customer,
a knight to save her but a figment of naïve imagination;
the men here,
rich in wallet but poor in soul,
who only lust after her supple body.

Alfonza looks at me,
she's beautiful and I'm a hypocrite,

her brown eyes a passport to fulfil my lost soul,
my lust.

She approaches.
I'm filled with temptation and excitement,
but why should I pay for a woman when I can
enjoy for free with my girlfriend;
more fool me who submits to my desires.

Can I buy you a drink,
I smile at Alfonza.

The Kino

I'm annoyed,
stressed,
my mind all over the place.

I see neon,
a sex show,
a kino.

Not been one before,
intrigued,
excited,
penis quickly inflated,
eyes dilated,
all over the place looking at G-strings and bras,
tits, ass and pussy on show.

Videos in kinos or live exhibition of double penetration;
hands inside trousers,
squeezing boobs.

I go to a private room humming,
baby oil shining,
grunting,
sex smelling,
heavy breathing,
sweating,
gyrating,
almost defibrillating,
cumming,
condom filling not face plastering.

I'm done.

The impulsiveness,
frustration,
boredom and anger,
drained

Back to the real world,
the usual,
the normal,
mundanity.

Half-an-hour of my life,
passed,
lived,
an experience not to be forgotten.

House Latina

I'm walking the crowded street,
on a high,
feel like I'm flying,
want to keep in the moment,
share my joy and fears,
with a someone,
a soulmate…
but there's no one I know.

Disappointed,
disjointed,
so much female temptation around…
but all frustratingly out of reach.

I spot a flashing sign,
"massage";
will I relax or get extras?

House Latina,
a house of ill repute,
a bordello where the sun rises as you finish with
a woman,
a whore house where I can release my pent-up
energy,
express my frustrations,
take out my disappointments.

My mind open and wallet full,
I don't hesitate,
don't think of repercussions,
only desire and lust.

I walk the creaking steps to the second floor,
knock on the innocuous door.

It's opened,
I'm greeted by a vision of vitality,
youth,
suppleness,
this in contrast to my aging years,
wearing body and greying temples…
but not my age-defying libido.

I'm in a sitting-room of lingerie,
five girls,
their assets on display,
boobs overflowing,
smiles and crossing of panty-less legs.

But it is the older,
quiet one in the corner,
the mischief in her eyes who gets my attention.

Long legs,
an ass that swallows her G-string,
a flat stomach,
two small bee stings,
a smile to die for,
crystal whites in dark chocolate.

She stands,
no words pass as she leads me down a corridor.
I'm not sure exactly what will transpire,
but have expectations,
liberations,
most likely further transactions,
ejaculations.

I enter a room,
space only for a bed but that's all we need.

Kick of shoes,
drop jeans,
remove shirt.

Unclothed,
disrobed,
I'm in my birthday suit.

I lie face down and wait,
wait for footsteps of my Latina,
our horizontal samba soon to dance.

The door closes,
candles are lit and music soothes.
She takes of panties and bra,
heats baby oil,
parts my legs,
caresses my feet her hands start to explore,
thighs,
buttocks rubbed,
squeezed,
her touch working their magic,
her hands rising up my body,
this as we chit-chat,
flirt
body-to-body massage we'll soon exert.

Her naked wondrous sits astride my hairy,
flabby tummy,
but she cares not as my dream turns to porn
reality,
this scenario,
an otherwise unlikely possibility.

Her nakedness envelops mine,
fingers air touch everywhere,
there is no innocence from this beatific beauty,
as nipples run up and down my body,
her legs caressing,
knees massaging my back.

I feel,
let all her small tender weight work my body
she,
pinning me down,
I,
letting her perform her craft,
her magic,
her expertise.

Turnover,
she smiles
I,
only too willing,
knowing she'll soon put out,

She goes to her knees,
takes me in her expert mouth,
sucking my hardness,
her light bush contacting my splayed fingers,
digits,
one,
two...
three inside her;
I feel her moistness,
wetness.

You want sex?
whispered.

She opens the condom packet with her teeth,
a bite she's made a thousand times.
She sheathes me,
gets on top and guides me in her lubed love
tunnel,
her body knowing how to move,
grind,
as she rides me,
experience of how to satisfy,
as I titties suck,
close eyes and cum.

Showered and reclothed,
I leave with a sense of wondrousness,
my every fibre confirming that was money well
spent,
a memory never forgotten but maybe repeated.

I leave the house of ill repute,
House Latina,
a bordello where the sun rises,
shafts of sunlight shining through the threadbare
curtains after I finish with my head-spinner;
truly,
this is the house of the rising sun.

Living our Truth

I'm in a place,
somewhere on my time space continuum,
working it out,
riding the waves of life,
the journey and not the destination...
all that bullshit.

Enough philosophical nonsense,
bromance,
just want romance,
a connection,
hopefully erection,

The meeting of minds not bodies my priority,
seniority,
there is no duopoly,
understanding this monopoly,
while looking to find happiness,
companionship,
humanity,
hopefully not paternity.

I have a drink,
look at girls
flirt with some,
get nowhere.

I see a woman,
looks dirty,
flirty,
much older than thirty,
nipples showing through shirty.

Big earrings,
blond hair,
blue eyes,
big boobs perfection,
my eyes drawn to her curvaceous derriere.
a firm,
sporty,
no visible panty line booty.

Lust on my mind,
chances of scoring,
low,
but fuck it,
I want to party,
to forget.

I imagine what it would be like to kiss,
clasp,
smack,
whip,
part and sink my tongue in her ass.

He twenty-year old body turns and catches me
staring,
drawling,
lustfully grinning.

Her fifty-year-old face smiles at me...
out of disdain?
Pity?
Excitement?
I can't tell,
I don't want to contemplate,
my mind oscillating between attempting to chat
her up and running.

Alright earrings?
I ask the dirty,
nipples showing through her shirty,
much older than thirty,
flirty MILF.
Can I buy you a drink?
I ask,
nothing wrong with such an approach,

She stares at me but doesn't say a word.

A cocktail?
I venture.
I want a long slow fuck,
she whispers,

her words caressing my ego,
tickling and twitching my manhood.

I'm speechless,
how do I proceed,
respond to that?

Sex on the beach,
I order from the barman,
She laughs,
I go crimson,
my confidence soars.

I take the drinks and sit next to her,
place my hand on her fabulous ass,
she,
letting me cup her gluttonous maximus.

I'm old enough to be your mum,
young man,
she saucily smiles.
Is this a rejection or offer?
I stay silent.

I'm 43 she says,
her hand grabbing my crotch.

I laugh,
my enjoyment obvious,
excitement poking up.
I'm 35, I lie,
I don't know why?

We chat,
talk.
It's honest,
no judgement,
her or me,
the opposite of my seven to three.

We leave together,
why shouldn't I party with Mrs dirty flirty?
be in another's' loving arms,
arms that I pay for brief intimacy,
someone who gives her body for money but not
her soul,
her heart to the work she does,
to the people she sleeps with.

Take your moral high ground...
but I need ground to steady my feet
earth to feed my soul.
I will change it up,
down or sideways,
live my true self,
temet nosce.

I, and the over thirty,
don't fabricate,
regurgitate,
placate,
but be innate,
both living our soul.

FRIENDS WITH BENEFITS

No man should be an island and all that. Social isolation has severe physical consequences, resulting in high blood pressure and an increased risk of heart disease and strokes. And this doesn't touch on the psychological effects of loneliness on the soul. As humans, we are wired for social interaction. Physiologically, being in a pack releases happy-smiley endorphins, this from our hunter-gatherer days. As such, answer me these questions three: Do you always feel better after sex? Are you fine with having sex that is not particularly meaningful love-making? Can sex be your escape from loneliness and the lack of love in your life? If you have answered "yes" three times, and have a friend that you like hanging out with but have no intention of forming a lasting partnership with, but you both like fucking… a friend with benefits could be the solution for both of oyu. However, getting into such a relationship, it's important to navigate such arrangements with care and consideration as once that rubicon is crossed boundaries will be blurred. Maybe one or both of you will consider, could he/she be the one for me, my forever as we develop deeper feelings and consider a longer-lasting partnership? Perhaps, you will conclude, another that got away? Will your friend with

benefits, be the person who you turn to when in need of a body to cuddle? What will you think if they get into a lasting relationship, get married, have children with someone else? Would you become insanely jealous of them and follow their life through the prism of social media hoping to detect in their smiles a distant look of longing? Will the sex always be exciting? Will you manage to go days or weeks without a phone call or WhatsApp message from them? Certainly, the dynamic will shift as circumstances change and complexities and challenges arise. Friends can come with benefits, but be careful with your heart and theirs! It's important to communicate openly and honestly about each others expectations, desires, and emotions.

Tuk-Tuk

The hum,
the drum,
the night starting to strum.

The beat,
the heat,
intoxicating.

The beer,
oh my dear,
what am I about to do?

The gin,
the sin,
there's never enough.

The whisky,
getting frisky;
time for some fun.

Add ice,
too much vice;
I'm losing control.

The band,
as I stand,
to dance the night fandango.

Dance,
gyrate,
almost ejaculate.

The night,
feels like flight,
as I arrive into tomorrow.

Enjoyed the bar,
take her to a car,
the night about to complete.

Rose

Part 1

You find me here,
now,
today,
this evening on our Tinder date.

You don't know my past,
my present,
we don't know the future,
just that was is and has been,
not that what is to be.

I'm a person of many colours,
influences good and bad,
insecurities and ego,
craziness and the mundane,
of worrying for others but needing to care for
myself,
mental more than physical.

I live each day one at a time not planning weeks,
months or lifetimes ahead,
life to much the victim of caprice,
avarice and hubris.

I'm married,
a father of four,
a complicated life liver.

I travel here to there,
more friends than family,
but I wouldn't change all that gone before,
this making me who you see today,
standing in front of you,
emotionally naked,
soul exposed,
living my truth,
there's no other way.

I can't,
wont hide,
lie out of pride,
but let you judge,
decide.

Know all or none of me,
this your choice,
my choice to know or not,
you;
are you a person I want to friend
or let brief encounters pass?

We are who we are,
why pretend else.
All fucked up lives,

complicated selves,
each living our rollercoaster.

Part 2

We met,
drank,
laughed,
held hands and shagged in toilets.

For 48 sweet hours we were together,
light in the other's darkness,
sharing hope when there was none.

I told you about another girl,
my infatuation with youth,
you are another level,
an independent woman,
brains and beauty,
so close but impossibly far away.

Life intervened,
your home is not mine,
your country not mine,
my wedding ring…
not given by you.

My neighbours plane seat did not have your
smile,
we both cast adrift,
fate to decide if we should meet again.

Messages shared,
thoughts explored,
anger sometimes uttered,
both wanting to know,
understand the other better no matter the distance.

Three months past those 48,
tonight we reunite.
Will two souls reconnect,
smiles broaden and bodies entangle,
or will the magic be dimmed by circumstance?

Part 3

I'm with my girl,
a night on the town as laughter and music ring
out,
beers consumed,
legs rubbed and lips kissed.

This is everything that I missed,
deeply miss,
a woman by my-side,
sharing fun and making new memories with you.

I'm not sure how the evening will finish,
what adventures my trouble-maker-in-chief will
get us into as we move bar to bar,
chat with strangers,
try drinks unknown,
do a boogie woogie.

We flirt with a girl,
take her to the dancefloor.
My fellow pirate holds her in front,
I grab waist from behind,
is this night just starting?

Have a threeway kiss in the taxi,
dreams about to become reality.
Back at the hotel,
the new girl leaves,
chickens out.
I'm disappointed until my woman,
my girl
my friend with benefits joins me hip to hip,
the night far from ending.

Part 4

I like you,
I really do,
soulmates is what you describe us as,
I wouldn't disagree.

I like your honesty,
openness,

that you let it all hang out;
I think I'm similar.

We both have a past,
my present,
wife and kids,
living in another country,
not a happy man despite all I have,
a complicated one.

I thought we were of like mind.
We have had fun together before,
in the bar and bed.
I was hoping for some few weeks of that when I
came...
mainly to visit you...
but,
it seems,
that I'm only your fuck toy,
not the soulmate you said.

Am I'm being used?
BTW...
this is what I like about you,
the honesty!

Did I have unreasonable expectations?
I totally get that you have your life,
your stresses and strains,
desires and hopes.

There are other men who can give you more than
I…
but going on dates when I'm here…
and just for a short time…
mainly to see you…
that's too much for me to handle,
not something a real soulmate would do.

I get it,
but wait until I leave.
I don't need to know about guys wanting to fuck you
when I'm hoping,
expecting,

it would be me,
us.

Here,
a fleeting few days,
you give to another.
Call me jealous,
not able to handle open relationships,
something we talked about.
Am I a hypocrite,
when the rubber meets the road,
I can't live by my words?

This is a head fucker-
wanting something,
someone I can't have.
I respect your life,
it's not my position to ask for something I can't give.

Rose,
I like you,
but life is emotionally easier as an island,
to fuck and forget,
to live the rollercoaster single,
the irony,
your freeness and certainty too much for me.

This is a motherfucker,
a real catch 22,
both of us rejoicing in the freedom of the other,
the core of who we are,
timing,
leading to emotions,
this is living,
God, you bastard!

I say with heavy heart,
Rose,
we can be friends if you want,
sex if things go that way,
wish each other luck,
keep in occasional touch,
maybe our ships will cross paths another time,
when we can really understand each other,
but for now,
47 goodbye.

Part 5

Who are you to me,
I to you?

We met,
chat and drink.
I slipped you one,
two and three more...
but was it just sex or a meetings of minds?

We are of different pasts,
uncertain presents,
who knows futures...
are ours intertwined?

Time and life keep us apart but we stay in touch,
somehow,
a Venn diagram of who the fuck knows what's,
a constellation we in the other's orbit,
thinking of similar Milky Ways.

Ours was a coming together of minds as much as
bodies,
of finding friendship in a lonely world,
both fighting inner demons,
the reality of the everyday,
of not having limitations or expectations,
living our truth.

But, who are you to me?
A sounding board?
Someone I can take my emotional and sexual
frustrations out on...
as much as you with me?

Who am I to you?

Are we living true selves in a cloaked world?
Many follow a false reality,
pretending because of expectations,
cultural, social and economical,
but living a lie?

In life there are too many questions,
no answers,
There are no certainties,
you someone who also understands this ambiguity,

that's why I like you,
why I don't know what to do with you.

Part 6

What should I do with you,
with me,
with us?
Is there an us or just a mess?

We are both broken,
both searching for lightening to strike-
maybe together,
maybe with others...
ours,
a relationship of…
convenience?
Friends with benefits?
Companionship?
All the above or none?
What we had I don't honestly know...
but I liked it.

When you cut our contact I understand why.
You didn't deserve the disrespect,
I,
hurt by your rejection,
ejection,
others intervening into business not theirs,
understanding,
not theirs.
but were you also looking for a way out,
a convenient excuse to break ties,
you moving on,
finding someone else to fill the hole in your life
that I couldn't?

Was I holding you back,
now you have a clear way forward,
I left bitter.

Life is not fair,
this we all know,
my life a little less without you in it,
my little Rose.
You my biggest conundrum!

Compersion

Life is far from simple,
each of us from 100s.
1,000s,
a million and more influences.

To see the best of me…
let me be me,
be happy for me,
let go of the me you thought I was,
that you want me to be.

My life is mine,
I want to share it with you,
to build on what we have,
to explore in what we are yet to uncover.

I am a person who wants to see new worlds and
people to meet.
Life is of wonderment,
to uncover the unknown,
explore the possibilities;
to be an experience collector.

We will argue and fight
be jealous and envious…
but can have more together than apart,
joy to share,
laugh together.

We can be two in one,
each knowing the other more than ourselves…
but, we are also different,
a unique life,
fears and hopes of our own.

Be with me on my journey
as I am on yours.
I don't want to be alone,
I want us to be there,
for each other,
to love and to understand,
to be happy in the other's happiness.

I hope you will find happiness in yourself
and us together,
you, my greatest friend with benefits

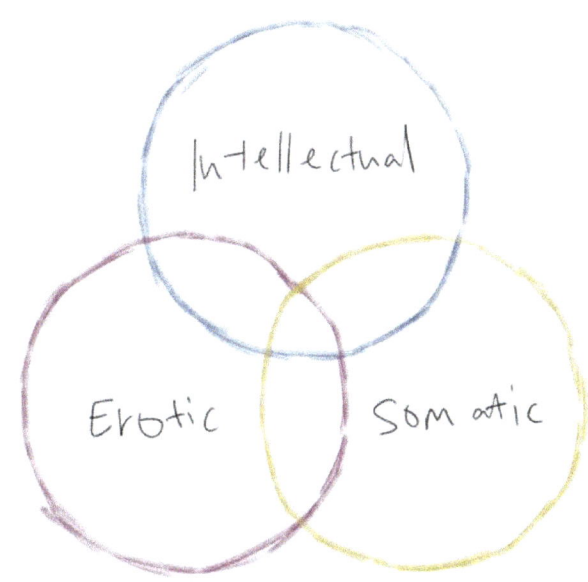

The Phone Interview

A Saturday morning...
my hands sticky,
I'm sweating,
brow clammy.

It wasn't planned,
but, one drink led to another,
to another,
to another,
into shots,
into strip poker;
what's there to say when you with your mate,
not girlfriend.

BEEP, BEEP, BEEP the alarm goes.
What day is it???
My bleary-eyed,
fuzzy brain asks.

The alarm goes again;
I'm dying.
Why?
I rack my brains,
and rack them again.

I'd seen an advert,
a dream job,
I the perfect candidate.
I applied,
this the interview.

I force myself from bed.
Shit, shave, shower, tea;
anything to feel alive.

Swaying and sweating,
I sit on the bed,
phone in hand,
my naked friend by my side,
an erection beneath my towel.

The phone rings,
hello, I say in my most professional voice.
Tell me about yourself.
Well, I started working at A, B and C,
I say by rote,
my brain slowly clicking into gear,
I managing to neither squeeze buttocks nor laugh
uncontrollably.

Having somehow talked coherently
for thirty minutes,
the interview ends.
I let out a sigh as I cum in her mouth.

Four weeks later,
I'm suited, booted and walking into my new
office
and ready to take on the world;
are they ready for me?

Am I in Heaven?

Its afternoon,
beers are drunk,
laughter had:
I'll be up all night.

Evening comes,
kebab consumed,
on to the rum and cokes;
I'll be up all night.

Light turns to dark,
bands listened to,
nightclub to follow;
I'll be up all night.

Set the dancefloor alight,
waists in hands,
living for the moment;
I'll be up all night.

In a taxi,
kissing lips,
hand up skirts,
us three,
we'll be up all night.

The Island

Have a fuck,
a fight,
kiss and make-up:
life's not shite.

We argue,
we cry,
we make love,
we die.

We two in one,
crazy and impetuousness,
envy and jealousness,
living for the morrow.

You my pole dancer,
I your foundation,
life is for living
we each other's resurrection.

We get a boat,
go island,
arguments left behind,
love reflate.

Captain Morgan shared,
biltong chewed,
crabs chased,
sea...
you getting screwed.

Memories made,
feeling alive,
feeling you,
feeling true.

We now leaving,
I dress wearing,
music hearing,
this been a great day with you.

Breaking Boundaries

We are friends
I knew that,
I thought you did too.

Friends with benefits,
defiantly,
understandably,
each other, secondary.

Hmmmmn!

So,
apparently we had different views,
ideas and expectations.

There were limitations,
thought I was clear,
now,
it's oh fucking dear,
this leading to confusion,
abusive fusion,
all round mental,
visceral contusion,
need urination,
take out my frustration,
not let be desperation,
destitution,
depression,
screw misappropriation,
I'm left is regression,
you,
leading me to emotional ruination.

I'm going on the warpath,
not the towpath,
this mutually assured destruction,
cos of your misguiding assertion,
blatant falsification,
ignorant misinformation that we were more than
friends with benefits.

Here comes a clarification,
I will not be objectification due to your fixation,
simplification,

Ghosting

My good friend,
we met,
drank, joked
and some good shagged;
fun times,
hoped for future shines.

I moved mountains,
literally,
to see you again.

Plans, I changed,
borders were crossed;
expectations for us,
to share weekends away…
maybe together would be forever?

I arrive,
call from the airport,
hope to hold you in my arms tonight.

You are cold on the phone,
no joy,
empty words,
platitudes and pleasantries,
a lack of conviction,
passion,
evident.

Talk one more time,
you inconclusive before vanishing,
abandoning our friendship,
not giving love a chance,
not giving me an explanation.

I understand your reality,
my life challengability,
I gave at least honesty,
deserved more than ghosting.

Around the World

Been around the world plenty,
not had for ages a hole,
that still sometimes the goal
I, hitting corner flag,
emotional sad,
lonely and bored,
needing connection,
not always reflection,
tired winless flirtation,
need penetration,
physical sensation,
body reunification,
bored of masturbation.

But still have hope,
right times will come,
I'll cum,
not emotional slum,
feeling eternally glum
alone like a clone,
no one noticing me,
wanting me…
unless financially abusing me.

Times will change,
friendship will win,
love will happen,
just have to keep the hope,
no more mope,
this not sexy,
turn off extray,
need changy
back in the game definitely,
this, liveability,
survivability,
mental revivability,
soon, I'll be unstopability and cool things to have,
do,
this, my universe,
once more,
I gravity.

A COMPLICATED LIFE

Navigating relationships and matters of fidelity can be challenging and emotionally charged. Whether an act constitutes cheating or not depends on the boundaries and agreements within a specific relationship. Different couples may have different expectations regarding monogamy and exclusivity. For instance, sometime back, I spotted an ex looking lonely and bored in a nightclub. She was in a group of girls and guys; no one seemed to give her much attention. I didn't think she had a boyfriend. I was smitten, drunk and horny, so went to chat to her. Is that cheating? Is that worthy of jealousy? I don't think so considering my current relationship is all but over, emotionally if not officially. Oh, to add, we did shag. So, even if I did cheat, I haven't really done anything wrong, have I? And besides, I bet my future ex has been getting a rod or two since we were last together!

It's certainly not only men who play the field. The reasons for infidelity can be complex and multifaceted. In the eyes of religion, the law of the land, or in matters of the heart, women are also cheaters. I'm sure ladies have just as many reasons to commit adultery, infidelity or wont a bit of naughty fun. It's enlightened times we live in and men's hearts can also be broken by their woman. So, now I've said it. Put the cat amongst the pigeons, the weasel in the rabbit hole, the squirrel amongst the ducks, the python up the Christmas tree and other images of animal chaos...

The Man's Perspective

Your smile,
the clothes extenuating your curves;
I'm enraptured.

Our skin touches,
you don't notice me,
but shivers go up my spine.

I, full of fantasies,
anticipation of the possibilities
living in hope to kiss your nakedness.

I stare at you.
Your legs crossed show thigh;
a queen on her throne.

I catch your dazzling brown eyes,
you coyly smile at me;
there's an animal attraction.

You continue talking to your friend,
a boy, a man;
someone not me.

I'm stuck to the spot in procrastination,
intimidated by rejection;
I, not good enough for you, an angel.

I drink for Dutch courage;
temptation and excitement in equal measure
flowing through my veins.

I cautiously approach
practice my chat up lines,
don't worry about wifey repercussions.

I'm lost in the moment,
not thinking what I will leave behind once the
rubicon crossed.

"Hi," you say.
I don't know how to reply.
"You want to dance?"

I have a stupendous smile on my face;
what new chapters will be written,
what new pleasures experienced?

I look into your brown eyes,
so different from the blue
that looked lovingly at me this morning.

I'm glued to the spot,
my heart leaping,
excitement at entering the unknown.

A Woman's Angle

No man can beat my man.
Hard worker, good looker.
faithful...
but boring.

I crave excitement,
to be treated like a princess,
noticed for who I am
not what I financially bring to a relationship.

A man is looking at me.
Floppy hair, broad shoulders,
square chin...
yummy!

Now he's staring.
Is it contempt, amusement, lust?
Is he mentally undressing me?
Can he reach places my man no longer goes?

A Mr Unpredictable, Mr Excitement,
a Prince Charming to whip me off my feet...
or just whip me,
make me climax a hundred,
a thousand times.

I look across the room and stare into his soul.
There is a chasm between desire and touch;
I want this forbidden fruit.

He swaggers over full of confidence,
Thinks I'll be an easy lay...
he'll be putty in my hands,
my mind tuned with desire.

He doesn't say a word.
He grabs my waist and pulls me into him.
I feel his hardness,
my legs turn to jelly.

I'm fulfilled being wanted.
It was this way at the beginning
with my husband,
Mr Predictable.

Sexual Frustration

We sleep together as friends not lovers,
we are no longer sexually free with each other…

Fantasies,
every perversion,
my unfulfilled dreams now only found on liq-
uid-crystal screen,
with battery operated friends.

Frustrated,
my sexual wishes are abandoned.
Why isn't my man willing to do that?
I silently ask as my hand goes up and down,
fingers in and out.

Is it me or him?
Does he not trust me,
love me anymore to give himself wholly?

Why does he not share my desires?
Why do I stay in a sexually unfulfilled marriage?

I want to stay faithful,
but…
my heart tells me that I only have one life,
that I'm getting older, greyer,
tummy loser,
boobs floppier,

that now is my last chance to be reckless,
feckless,
to have no regrets,
to live my fantasies,
pay if I must.

Sex,
my weakness,
my impulsivity,
to forget real world consequences
when hopping bed-to-bed,
living a parallel life to my betrothed.
as I need to feel desired,
fulfilled.

Night Adventure

Its afternoon,
beers are being drunk,
laughter had;
I will be up all night.

But inside,
I'm depressed,
the home front tricky,
I'm getting close to icky.
my life about to crash.

I know why I drink,
to forget my mistakes,
to create something out of nothing,
to engage with those equally lost,
alcohol our mutual oil
the grease to let sun follow the moon.

I remember all the good I have left behind,
I feel so melancholy,
my past a millions miles,
a thousand universes from here,
I,
a lost planet amongst a trillion stars.

Evening comes,
kebab consumed,
on to the rum and cokes;
I'm certain to drink all night.

The present unfolding,
the future unknown,
living life large;
I'm drunk,
this a statement of fun and fact!

I'm having a beer,
karaoke called,
I turn,
stumble,
smack my knee on step.

Light turns to dark,
bands listened to,
nightclub to follow.

Been a good night,
time to move on,
no falling into a fug while I walk.
no sleeping on the tram;
I will do anything,
another beer,
a water,
coke,
anything to keep awake,
to keep the party going and demons away;
I can keep up all night.

I know where I'm going,
but quickly eyes closing,
trying to keep open,
music blasting through earphones,
slap myself on the face;
keep brain alert,
a facade of decency;
DON'T fall asleep!

Give into temptation,
tube stop missed,
mobile phone stolen.
head lolling side-to-side,
my drunken reality.

I wake,
pass a station never seen before,
lost,
shrug my shoulders,
get off,
leave,
walk in the hope to find salvation,
a party where I can dance till sunrise as I don't
want to,
can't admit defeat,
to accept that I brought troubles on myself,

that I'm reckless,
heartless,
soon wifeless,
my indiscretions unforgivable.

I must learn to forgive myself,
that all the shit that happens in this world is not
all down to me,
that I'm not the conductor of chaos in the lives
of those I care for,
that no more can I stop ripples in a pond,
of my decisions,
than from the sun shining.
I,
but one of billions with a cross to bear.

I hear music,
the African beat that is so resoundingly familiar,
I don't know how I got here,
but I'm not worrying.

Start chatting to a princess.
You're black,
he's yellow,
she's brown and I'm white.

Maybe you think life is easy for me,
a heterosexual white man,
married man,
but all the advantages in the world are not mine,

I'm not the start or finish of all your problems or
solutions.
I'm not my forefathers,
I can't change my genetics,
lineage,
parents or cultural heritage…

Like you,
I'm simply all of what has brought me here,
to this time and place,
I start,
drunken words tumbling out my mouth.

Do not make your race,
religion,
sexuality,
marriage define you,
she says to me.

Life is far more complicated than that
we are all more interesting than labels.
You don't know who I am or where I've come
from,
you don't know of my success of failures,
my enjoyments or heartache,
what makes me crazy in life,
love or friendship.

Serendipity has brought us to this point in time,
let's enjoy ourselves,
not worry what others say,
but live in the moment.
each with our prejudices and insecurities
this what makes us who we are.

Together,
we are strangers in a strange land,
this nightclub,
a new home away from home,
we both lost in a sea of language unknown,

customs unrecognizable,
culture so different to what we are accustomed…
but this is what we live for,
the challenge of adoption,
absorption,
assimilation,
to learn the unknown and experience new tastes
and sights,
make new friends,
this city once indecipherable now well known,
new home,
I just need,
not be alone.

We finish talking,
drinking,
enjoying the other's groove,
now is the time to set the dancefloor on fire.

My hands clasp her waist,
my hips pressed into her apple,
she pushing back to feel my grind,
my knife finding her pips,
together living for the moment;
we will be up all night.

Let's go,
she says,

her smile leaving no doubt what's next.
Sure,
I reply nonchalantly,
my erection not able to hide my desire.

In a taxi we get,
she's not asked for my address,
I've no idea where we will go,
where she lives,
what her flat looks like,
does she live alone and we can fuck in every
room….
or is she also married?

The car comes to a halt,
lips untangle,
her hand comes out from my trousers,
I do up buttons after my fingers leave her panties;
we will definitely be up all night!
You pay,
I'm told,
a ride home the price for her body,
hopefully soul,
this, I'm more than willing to reach into my wallet.

Why Do I Make Life Hellishly Complicated?

Steady wife,
steady life,
steady work,
just got a 30-year mortgage…
no excitement,
no living on the edge,
no vivaciousness in life;
the elixir run dry.

Am I still important to you,
my wife?
Why?
What do you need me for?
Money, is that it,
is that all I am to you?

I feel no love,
otherwise you would hear my cries for us,
me,
we.

You care not to heal this crisis,
no longer do you share your hurts,
hopes and fears with me;
we are both in a world of one.

Why have you given up on me,
us?
Why am I so unimportant to you?
You no longer show me your true self!
It seems that I'm only a hassle to you,
your actions speaking louder than words;
it kills me,
killing us.

You have made your decision to not share your
thoughts,
your life with me.
To give answers as to why you run away from me.
Why you no longer want me as part of your life.

If you won't say it,
I will,
there's nothing left between us apart from our
marriage certificate.

We were in love,
lust,
but life has taken that,
turned it to dust.

Desire,
no longer enough to keep us together.
My fixation,
now,
to be elsewhere,
with someone else,
this,
stronger than to keep me with you,
unloved and feeling lost.

And so,
I venture into the night,
the unknown,
this my choice,
my decision to adventure alone.

I enter a bar.
This should not be my place,
not my time,
I'm here by circumstance to pass minutes away…
but the fug that greets me,
the haze,
smell,
sight,
the attack on the senses that's so familiar
is like a warm embrace.
This could be a night of revelry,
happiness and joy,
just what I require.

I look and see smiling faces
and dancing bodies.
My mind is confused,
lonely;
I have no soul to jive with.

I have some booze,
my elixir,
manic sauce to enliven my mojo,
turn me into superman,
where anything and everything is possible.

I see a smile,
We start talking,
flirting,
all I want knowing,
where will I sleep tonight,
I need love,
not never-ending fight.

Master of Disaster

Horny but defeated,
castrated,
constipated;
I'm a master of disaster,
can't get it up,
this time not a cum blaster.

I love my woman,
wifey,
want to make love to her,
sex,
fuck,
she is my life;
the mind willing,
the Colonel ain't.

I'm not the first visitor to my lover's body this
month,
nor the most attractive,
rich,
funny or big dicked.

I can't do sexual gymnastics.
I'm not a comedian,
billionaire,
Casanova,
porn star or genius;
I'm me,
an ordinary bloke
with an extraordinary woman
who for some reason smiles at me,
is naked with me,
is disappointed by me…
I, her pity because I'm now ordinary for her,
that I don't measure up to lovers,
this purgatory!

Misunderstood

I'm not the principal,
but do have principles,
my motivations and ethics now being questioned.

I'm a school teacher,
economics my subject,
eduction my constituency.

A life of 73 years,
many shared underage beers,
debuted 45 years back,
now being put on the morality rack.

How many A Levels paased,
boys helped,
sherries is what I gave boarders,
family nest they left.

I filled their void with other intentions,
my school,
lots of gossip no recriminations.

I've been shamed but am shameless,
I blameless,
the youth nameless so many I tried,
all the time,
plain sight I hide.

Literature I used to give,
all the time thinking,

this not how to live,
my libido for youth left frustrating.

This life I was playing at,
being upstanding not a twat,
not the real me,
I like young boys and needed to be free.

I'm not a queer,
just an old dear,
a lifetime of no,
but here to prison I go.

Pussy So Good

There was a girl I knew,
who knew a song or two;
her hair went from blonde to bald,
her mind silver to gold

Her interests changed,
girl to boy,
my like for her;
I can't keep untold.

Do you want me?
she asked;
my heart said, yes,
my married brain couldn't be arsed.

We lived apart,
life working that way;
be together again,
I hoped one day.

She told me:
I ain't got cash,
but a nice,
tight,
wet,
money-making gash;
my pussy so good,
it's an ATM machine.

She exuded sex,
my nether regions twitched.
I said to her,
roses are red,
violets are blue,
so is my cock,
I'm going to stick it in you!

We fucked like rabbits and ass to mouth,
I quickly forgot about my soon to be ex,
and came in her mouth.

I stopped reflecting,
as she started cum gurgling;
next it was my time,
I licked pussy squirting.

I was in love with this girl,
and all her kinky stuff;
perhaps this time,
together means forever and all that lovey-dovey
fluff.

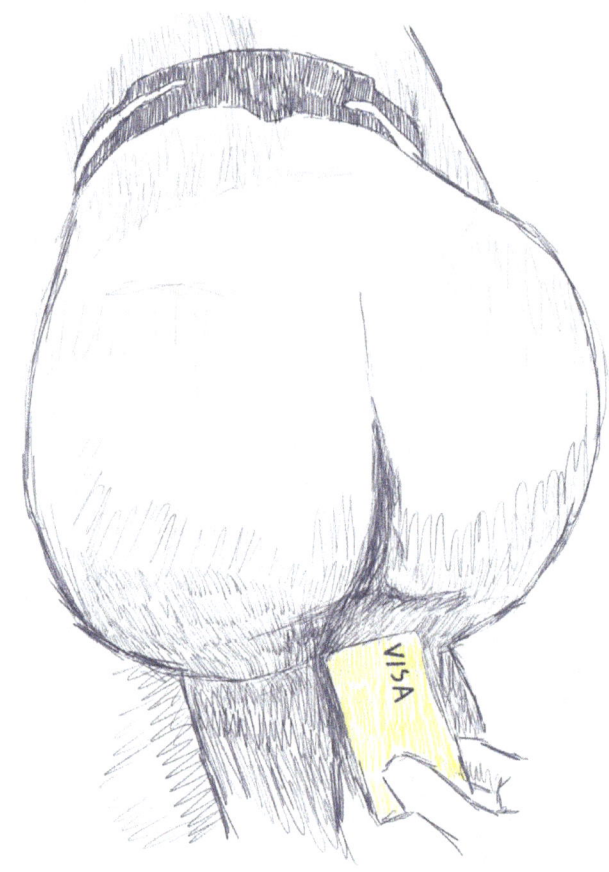

Allegedly

A judge, a jury,
but no defendant;
finding someone guilty,
but without conviction for confrontation.

Is someone guilty of philandering…
or just malicious gossip?
Guilty of wrongdoing…
or not knowing all the facts?
Someone who says, allegedly,
I allege, they are cowards.

A woman was walking down the street…
she saw a postman coming out her neighbour's
house,
she alleged, they were having an affair.
The postman's wife divorced him on this allega-
tion;
a true story,
but not a real affair.

Why do people use the word, allegedly?
Is it to feel important,
powerful?
To be considered the master or mistress of all
knowledge when they don't have all the facts?

Don't allege,
be forthright;
in this life and the next,
your word is your honour.

A FINAL THOUGHT

Throughout my live, the women I have met have raised thought-provoking questions and emotions about my morality, ethics, way of living, motivations and the meaning of love. I now not only question myself about big important shit but also the minutiae. I no longer question whether I should move out of the shadow of obliviousness and ignorance but know I should search for answers I do not yet understand, as what may be uninteresting to you, is a world of unexplored possibilities to me.

Sex carries profound significance. It is elemental, a core component of our being. It is literally how we become. This is what I've learned from going round the block a few times. Firstly, you (meaning me) will either be in a state of sexual satisfaction or frustration. There is no middle ground. There has to be compromise with your partner and understand that what might be good for one is not necessarily what the other wants. You somehow have to find a way that both parties are comfortable with. The second point, is, with your partner – whether in life or a one-night stand – you need to have at least two of the following five. I call these my Five Fucking Follows. 1) Be Friends or lovers (though strangers can be good as well). 2) Be Fatally attracted to your fuck fellow. 3) Fulfilment, the sex should be satisfying for both parties. 4) Frequency, is it often enough? 5) And most importantly, it should be Fun. On a one-night stand, by definition you are likely to get two if not more of these five, but the challenge is in a long-term relationship. You need to be sexually satisfied otherwise you will end up frustrated. The problem comes when looking at your sex life and if only one (if even that) of these five boxes are being ticked. If that is a case, you need to look at the fundamentals of what is keeping you together and how to address the challenges. In summary, when it comes to rolling around in the sheets or shagging in the sea, find someone who you are physically, emotionally and sexually compatible with. Having open communication, understanding, and a willingness to explore and fulfil each other's needs will all contribute to a satisfying and fulfilling sexual relationship.

Thank you, dear reader, my friend for being on this poetic journey. I hope through my experiences I have given you a new perspective on life. So, I say, never blame your circumstances. A positive mind-set will always lead to a more fortuitous outcome than a negative approach. One should not fear failure; it happens- get up and give it another lash. Don't be ashamed of your mistakes; learn from them. We all screw-up, accept this is part of life. Embrace experience, good or bad; there is always something to be learned. If you don't go after what you want, you will never have it. If you don't ask, the answer is always no. If you don't step forward, you will remain in the same place. Be curious and have a willingness to engage with the unknown. Questioning does not show weakness but is rather a sign of strength, a true measure of intelligence. Open yourself to the world and express that you aren't afraid to exhibit your ignorance but want to learn, search for knowledge and truth from those who can educate and guide. "By doubting we are led to question, by questioning we arrive at the truth." Peter Abelard, 1079- 1142

Nirvana

Chatting,
flirting,
think romancing,
aiming for undressing.

In the taxi hands explore,
tongues touch,
erection gets,
wetness starts.

Unlock the front door,
fumble and squeeze,
lift up dress,
pull down trousers,
we a pair of arousers.

Turn around and bend over,
do the superman,
cowgirl,
doggy after missionary,
every position a climax strategy.

Exhausted,
sweating,

smiling,
now the time for mind exploring calmly,
lovingly,
feel body tenderly.

Re-join at the hip,
moment of seconds,
minutes like hours,
two souls thinking as one;
nirvana.

ABOUT THE AUTHOR

I'm an entrepreneur & business consultant by day, novelist & poet by night. The son of a British Army officer, I volunteered in rural Tanzania in 1997 before going to university to study marketing. I have lived and worked in Ethiopia, Germany, Kenya, Jordan, Ireland, Malawi, Saudi Arabia, Tanzania and the UK over the last 25 years, my varied experiences of culture, relationships, food, music and everything else that makes the world go round, the source of my inspiration.
zania and the UK over the last 25 years, my varied experiences of culture, relationships, food, music and everything else that makes the world go round, the source of my inspiration.

www.ingramcontent.com/pod-product-compliance
Lightning Source LLC
Chambersburg PA
CBHW081207170626
46811CB00011B/3339